TENDER

Story By: Jason Van Geem
Illustrations by: Jason Van Geem

By: Jason Van Geem

DEDICATION

This book is dedicated to my Mother and Father who have always inspired me to be creative and to my wife and son, you both motivate me everyday and I love you guys.

PREFACE:

This book was written to entertain and teach a valuable lesson about being who you are and finding your place. I hope you enjoy the stories of Tender and friends. He's an ambitious skunk who sees opportunity in the world, and sets out to accomplish his goals.

Deep in the woods there lived a happy little Skunk named Tender and he played with his skunk friends all day. Tender and his friends would not have it any other way. They all played games so smelly and proud, in their little forest where others weren't allowed.

One day, Tender accidentally roamed into a family's backyard, where he saw a boy and girl playing with their puppy from a far. "Wow!" Thought Tender, "A family to play with can be so much fun. Hopefully one day I'll be a family's special number one!" From that day on Tender wanted to be a family pet skunk, but that was very hard to do because of how badly he stunk.

Most animals like dogs and cats are easily chosen to become a house pet, but families don't care to own a smelly skunk and that you can bet. Tender was saddened by this horrible news, so he went to talk with his other animal friends for help and some clues.

At first he talked with his close friend, Bruno the skunk, but he couldn't help pull Tender out of his slumped little funk. "We're not meant to be house pets my dearest old friend, the skunk is a wild smelly animal and it will be till the end." "I don't believe this" claimed Tender with might, but was Tender wrong or could he be right? "To beat the odds is what I'm about and soon I'll join a family and prove you wrong in your doubt."

So Tender set off to find his first words of advice, of how to join a family that was caring and nice. He met his good his friend, Cammie the cuddly kitten, to help him on his way, so he could be with a good family hopefully one day. "It's all about being cozy, cuddly and cute. To purr and meow that is the best route." Tender didn't know how to be cozy, cuddly or cute, he only knew how to squander and be smelly like toot.

Next Tender went to visit his jazzy reptilian friend, Luis the Laughing Lizard, who enjoyed the heat and avoided all blizzards. He sat on his hot rock and listened to Tender and then thought of advice to make of good splendor. "It is not about cuteness or cuddles or cozies, it's about jazzy personality with quickness and mosey."

"Mosey?" Asked Tender, who did not understand? "Yes, mosey my friend, it's strolling with confidence along the hot sand." "But I am not Mosey nor jazzy at all." "Well then you are no lizard Mr. Wizard, and a family skunk is not a good call. Perhaps Bleaky can help who is so very wise. Perhaps he has the answer with his googly eyes."

On his way to see Bleaky, Tender meets a beautiful
little girl with golden freckles and glasses that hung on
the tip of her nose. "Hello little skunk, what is your
name?" "My name is Tender." He happily replies with so
much joy in his eyes. "My name is Amy May and I really
like skunks, but my family does not." With this news
Tender's heart had sunk.

"But maybe they'll like you? Let's give it a try. Come to the house, do not be shy." Tender went off with Amy to meet her parents at home, but when dad smelled the air and knew Tender was there, he said, "no way!" and let out a groan!

Later on, Tender finds Bleaky, his brilliant buzzard pal, who would not fly because being up in the air was just too high. The ground level was fine, just fine indeed, especially for this brainier bird that did love to read. "You see my good friend your problem is odor, the smell is too foul and I'll need my decoder. If I can fix the stench so you no longer stink, you'll be with that family in less than a blink. Now let's see where did I place it, or put it, it's missing? No! The honeycomb piece in it is broken and hissing! I cannot fix you my gentle friend. I'm now at a loss, unless you can get me one from those wiggling wasps."

On his way to the wasp's nest, Tender runs into Francis, a fool hearted ferret that takes incredible chances. "Hey Tender! Where are you heading today?" Asks Francis. "Off to the wasps nest to get a honeycomb part for Bleaky's machine that will not start." "Can I come along and join in on the fun!?" Exclaimed Francis who was ready to run. "Sure, but be careful these wasps are quite mad, if they give us a sting, it could be quite bad."

During their walk Tender asks Francis how to be a house pet. "Cammie said to be cute and Luis said it was mosey, but I am not jazzy nor am I cozy." Francis ponders for a moment, "Hmm, well my fur has colors and you're black and white, that could be something that's sore for their sight? Plus, I'm a ferret who's goofy you see, that's one trick that has worked well for me!" "I can be goofy and stand on my head and paint my white stripe to a new color red," said Tender.

They step off the trail and paint Tender's stripe. He acts like a goofball, but can't get it right. CRASH! He stumbles into the cans! The paint splatters off the white stripe and all over his fur, now he's a mess, a big mess for sure.

Once again, Tender feels defeated, but onward to the honeycombs that are very much needed. "I see them!" Yells Francis with much excitement and delight. "But how do we get them? These wasps give me such fright!" "I have a plan!" Said Tender. "I'll distract them with my scent and then you move in as quick as you can, but you have to be quick or be stung on the hand."

Both Tender and Francis got into place and then Tender sprayed his scent into their face. The wasps buzzed around in mass disarray, as Francis snagged a honeycomb...Hip! Hip! Hooray!

Bleaky adds the honeycomb piece to the decoder, with a tweak here or there, he has a new odor! As Tender was about to go, leaving his old self behind, Bleaky spoke up with concern on his mind. "But Tender, you're different, you're just not yourself. I miss your white stripe and your skunk scent throughout. A family that will love you for your special traits, is a family worth being with, one that is great!" Tender stood for moment and thought about what Bleaky had said, and so he changed back to his usual self.

Amy finds tender in the park with all of his friends. "Tender come quick, I've got such good news! My family will let you stay, they've agreed if you choose. My dad said okay after I begged and I pleaded, and as it turns out you're very much needed. I told him about how you dealt with the wasps and made them go far away. Well we have wasps that are trying to stay." Tender was so happy he jumped and smiled, he found a good family and could be himself all the while. He was the happiest skunk forever and ever, and he didn't

have to try to be cozy or cute, or jazzy or brown, he
was just sweet little Tender all the way around.

THE END

Please Check out other works by
Jason:
Rudy: The Rocket Ship

www.ingramcontent.com/pod-product-compliance
Lightning Source LLC
Chambersburg PA
CBHW041613120626
46551CB00002B/421